Starring Katy Duck

By Alyssa Satin Capucilli   Illustrated by Henry Cole

Ready-to-Read

SIMON SPOTLIGHT

New York   London   Toronto   Sydney   New Delhi

For Peter, Laura, and Billy, my dancing stars!—A. S. C.

Katy Duck loves to dance. She loves to bend. She loves to twirl like a leaf. "Tra-la-la. Quack! Quack!"

Katy Duck loves to dance
in the morning.
She loves to dance in
the afternoon.

Most of all, Katy loves
to dance under a starry sky.
"Tra-la-la! Quack! Quack!"

Katy leaps and twirls.

Then Mrs. Duck says,

"Time for bed, Katy Duck."

Katy Duck dreams of
dancing on a great stage.
"Bravo!" cheers the crowd.
"Bravo, Katy Duck!"

The next day at dance class
Mr. Tutu says,
"I have a great surprise.
We are having a dance
show!"

Katy Duck is very excited.

She can hardly believe it.

What a dream come true!

"Tra-la-la! Quack! Quack!"

Each day, Katy and her class practice and practice.

They dance in the morning and in the afternoon.

Every night at home, Katy
dances under a starry sky.

At last it is time for
the big show!
There is a great stage.
There are pretty costumes.

"Places everyone!"
says Mr. Tutu.
"Take your places, please!
The show is about to begin."

The curtain opens.
There are bright lights.
There is an audience . . .
with lots of people.

Katy Duck feels shy.

Very shy.

"Tra-la-la! Gulp! Gulp!"

The music begins.

Katy Duck looks right.

The other dancers nod.

Katy Duck looks left.

Mr. Tutu smiles.

Then Katy Duck looks up.

The lights on the stage twinkle.

The lights look just like the starry sky!

Katy loves to dance under the starry sky.

Katy feels her arms
start to flutter.
Her feet begin to
pitter patter.

Katy Duck leaps and twirls!
She stretches and sways
to the music.

Dancing under the bright
lights is fun!

"Bravo!" cheers the crowd.

"Bravo, dancers!"

"Bravo, Katy Duck!"
says the crowd.

Dancing on the great stage
is just like Katy dreamed.

"Tra-la-la! Quack! Quack!
How I love to dance!"
says Katy Duck.

Katy Duck,
Flower Girl

For Dave and Kristin, *Tanti auguri*, always . . .
—A. S. C.

"I have wonderful news,"
Mrs. Duck told Katy Duck.
"Aunt Ella is getting
married!"

"At the wedding, Emmett will carry the rings. You will be the flower girl, Katy," said Mrs. Duck.

"Tra-la-la. Quack! Quack!"

A wedding? A flower girl?

Katy Duck was so excited!

"I must practice,"
said Katy.
Outside, Katy Duck
swayed like a daffodil
in the breeze.

She stretched like a
tulip in the sun.
She could hardly wait
to be a flower girl.

At last, it was time
for the wedding.

"Come along, Katy,"
said Mrs. Duck.
"We must get ready."

First, Mrs. Duck
dressed Emmett.
Katy thought he looked
a bit like Mr. Duck.

Then Mrs. Duck
helped Aunt Ella.
Katy had never seen
anyone so beautiful!

"Now it is your turn, Katy,"
said Mrs. Duck.

Katy Duck closed her eyes.
She took a deep breath.

"Tra-la-la. Oh no!"
cried Katy Duck.
"That dress does not
look like a flower at all."

"Oh, Katy," said Mrs. Duck.
"A flower girl does not
look like a flower."

"A flower girl **tosses** flowers at a wedding!" said Mrs. Duck.
Katy looked down.

"But maybe **this** flower
girl can dance like a
flower too!" Aunt Ella said.
Now Katy smiled.

The music began.
Emmett carried the rings
very carefully.
He looked proud!

"You're next, Katy,"
Aunt Ella said
with a smile.
She gave Katy a big hug.

Katy tossed flower petals to her left.

She tossed them to her right.

And as the music soared,
Katy Duck swayed
like a daffodil and
stretched like a tulip.

Everyone agreed she was
a wonderful flower girl.

"Tra-la-la. Quack! Quack!
How I love to dance!"
said Katy Duck.

"Tra-la-la. Quack! Quack!
How I do love
a wedding, too!"

Katy Duck
Goes to Work

For all the wonderful moms and dads who
bring their children to work . . . including my own!
— A. S. C.

"Today is a special day, Katy," said Mrs. Duck. "You are going to work with Dad!"

"Tra-la-la. Quack! Quack!"
Katy was so excited.
She had never gone to
work before.

Katy chose her best tutu.
She put on her boa and
a sparkly crown.

Then Katy danced
into the living room.
Katy Duck loved to dance.

"Tra-la-la. Quack! Quack!
I am ready for work!"
she said.

Katy leaped and spun
all the way to the
bus stop.

She looked out
the bus window.
The trees swayed
like ballerinas!

It was a busy day at work
for Katy Duck.

Katy typed.

She pressed lots of buttons.

She visited the watercooler.

She colored with crayons.

"Tra-la-la. Quack! Quack!
Work is fun," said Katy.
"But not as much fun
as dancing!"

Katy whirled.

She pranced.

She twirled.

"Tra-la-la. Quack! Quack!"
Katy danced here.

Katy danced there.

"Tra-la-la—"

BUMP! THUMP!

Katy sent papers flying everywhere!

"Oh no, Katy,"
said Mr. Duck.
He looked upset.

Very upset.

Katy looked right.
Katy looked left.
Katy looked down.

"Now, now, Katy,"
said Mr. Duck.

"I know you love to dance.
But at work, you must
dance a bit more carefully.
Okay?"

Katy nodded.

She helped Mr. Duck

clean up the papers.

Then she helped Mr. Duck
order lunch.
They even shared an
ice-cream sundae!

"Tra-la-la. Quack! Quack! How I love ice cream," said Katy Duck.

"Tra-la-la. Quack! Quack!
And how I love going
to work with you,"
she said.

Mr. Duck smiled and
gave Katy a spin.
"Tra-la-la. Wheee!"
They danced all the way
home.

Katy Duck

Makes a Friend

Katy Duck loves to
dance.
"Tra-la-la.
Quack! Quack!"

Katy Duck loves to dance
with her brother, Emmett.
"Tra-la-la.
Quack! Quack!"

Katy leaps and twirls.
Emmett jumps and
bumps.

Soon Mrs. Duck says,
"It is time for a nap,
Emmett."

"Tra-la-la. Boo-hoo,"
says Katy.
"Who can I dance with
now?"

Just then the doorbell
rings! "That must be
our new neighbor,"
says Mrs. Duck.

"I hope our new neighbor
loves to dance,"
says Katy Duck.

Katy Duck opens
the door.
She does her
best curtsy!

"Hello! My name is Katy Duck. I love to dance!

Tra-la-la!

Quack! Quack!"

"I am Ralph.
I love things that
go fast."

"I love cars.

I love airplanes.

I love rocket ships.

Zip! Zoom! Whoo-oo-sh!"

Katy Duck looks to
her left.
"Do you like to dance?"
asks Katy.

Ralph looks to his right. "Do you like things that go fast?" he asks.

Katy and Ralph look down. "There must be something we both like to do," says Katy Duck.

"But what?" asks Ralph.

Katy and
Ralph
think and
think.

They think
and think
some more.

"I know!" says Katy
Duck. She flaps her
arms up and down.
Katy zips.
Katy zooms.

"Look at me, Ralph! I am an airplane! Tra-la-la. Quack! Whee!" says Katy Duck.

"10-9-8-7-6-5-4-3-2-1 . . .
BLAST OFF!" shouts
Ralph.

"I am a rocket ship."

"Me too! BLAST OFF!" says Katy Duck.

"This is fun!" says Ralph.

They zip and zoom.

They whirl and twirl.

"How I love to dance," says Katy Duck.

"Especially with a new
friend like you, Ralph.
Tra-la-la.
Quack! Quack!"

Katy Duck
and the
Tip-Top Tap Shoes

For my most tip-top editor, Valerie, with love!
—A. S. C.

There was a new duck
in dance class.
Katy Duck wanted
to meet her!

"Tra-la-la. Quack! Quack!
My name is Katy Duck.
I love to dance."

"Tra-la-la. Tap! Tap!
My name is Alice Duck.
I love to dance too."

The music began.
Katy felt her arms flutter.
Her feet began to
pitter-patter.

Tip-top-tap!

Tip-top-tap!

What was that sound?

Tap! Tap! Tap!

It was Alice Duck!

Alice Duck had tap shoes.

The tap shoes were black.

They were very shiny.

They made tapping sounds!

Tap! Tap! Tap!

"Stop the music," called
Mr. Tutu.
"Stop the music,
please!"

"Now, now, " said Mr. Tutu.
"You do not need tap
shoes in here, Alice.
This is ballet class."

"Tra-la-la. Tap! Tap!
But I love my tap shoes,"
said Alice.

Alice tapped here.

Alice tapped there.

"My tap shoes are tip-top!"

Mr. Tutu rubbed his chin.

The class grew quiet.

Katy Duck looked right.

She looked left.

"Wait!" said Katy Duck.
"I have an idea.
You can try my extra
slippers!"

"You can float
like a swan.
And sway like a flower.

You can wear your
tip-top tap shoes
after ballet class."

Alice looked down at her
shiny tap shoes.
She looked at Katy's
soft slippers.

"That sounds like a
tip-top idea to me!"
said Alice Duck.

Alice and Katy stretched high. They bent low.

After class,
Alice asked Katy,
"Would you like to
try my tap shoes?"

"Oh yes!" said Katy.

Tip-top-tap!

Tip-top-tap!

"Tap shoes are fun!"

Alice swayed. She floated.
"Ballet slippers are fun
too," said Alice Duck.

"Tra-la-la. Tap! Tap!
Tra-la-la. Quack! Quack!
How we **love** to dance!"